"She."
A poetry series by:
Isabelle Alerte;

1. ORIGIN;
2. WHAT SHE WANTED TO SAY;
3. HER;
4. HIM;

1. Daze

I've been told you love me a hundred times.
I've been promised oceans and moons and stars.
As long as I waited for its arrival.
Never received not one,
I guess those were all lies.
Smiles that never stretched for me.
Eyes that longed for me,
Only when yours were filled with lust.
And I day dreamed a reality that wasn't real.
Where your love meant more than words,
And your touch took me to other worlds.
A reality where an us would work.
And I day dreamed you loving me for some years,
But it wasn't reality.
Something I made up in desperation.
In desperation of wanting your love.
Not even necessarily your love,
But your friendship and your presence.
And your very being and essence.
I made up this reality because I was in love.
I had told you hundreds of times that I was.
I had nothing to offer to you,

I knew I was a liability to you.
So I promised you my loyalty,
And gave you my heart.
In hopes that I'd keep hearing that you love me.
In hopes that you'd keep smiling at me.
In hopes that you'd still see me,
With love filled Eyes.
My day dreams blurred reality.
Reality where I am a liability.
Reality where you tell me you love me,
And I believe it and you know that I do.
Reality where you say you love me,
Just to keep me from leaving you.
Reality where you say it but don't mean it,
But I don't hear the underlying underneath it.
I welded my ears shut to the idea.
But I don't see it,
Because my eyes won't believe it.
They're rolled back,
Stuck day dreaming,
In love with you.

2. Underlying Truth.

Tell me no.
Tell me your love is selfish and that you cannot
Share with me.
Tell me that you stopped listening,
Not because you couldn't hear me,
But because you realized,
I wasn't worth listening.
Tell me you need me to leave,
That I'm not wanted here.
Tell me I'm the problem,
And there's no future where you see me in it.
Tell me you can do better.
Tell me it was just a joke that you took too far,
And you're ready for it to be over.
Tell me you don't want me,
That you never did.
Tell me that every time your eyes,
Laid upon mine,
They trailed down to my body,
And that you never looked back up.
That you only loved to look at my figure,
But not what was inside.

That you wanted to explore my skin.
Not because I trusted you enough to do so,
But because it brought you self-pleasure.
My pleasure was just in addition.
Tell me you used me to satisfy your lust.
That it was just lust that you used me for.
Tell me there was never love.
Tell me and then tell me again.
So that I can see the image that you see.
So that I can paint the picture,
Like Picasso to detail.
So that I can paint the picture without me in it.
That you'd look at it and agree.
That there was never any love for me.
Tell me your underlying truth,
So that I can see it as my truth.
That I'm not needed.
The picture was perfect with just you.

3. Self to Self Conversations:

You realize how disturbing your thoughts are?
Do you realize how loud you're being??
KEEP IT DOWN!
I'm trying to live.
I swear if I even hear another peep from you,
I'm sending you away.
Like the last time.
The last, last time.
And all the other time's before then.
Think I won't?
You thought your thoughts were coveted?
Thought I couldn't reach them?
You're putting me down.
You in-functional little shit.
You're depleting me of life.
You're stealing part of my lungs.
You're trying to become my voice.
You're not stronger than I.
You're just my mental.
I'm the physical,
With physical strength.
That's why you're just the voice in my head.

You stole half my heart.
And left me with the basics.
Told me survive somehow.
Without my mental.
You told me to survive with just my physical.
Cause you'd given up on holding your end.
Too much physical labor for you.
So you sit and pretend.
And contemplate and think.
And drove me crazy,
How could you???
You're me but not really.
Just the voice inside my head.
That yells that life is over.
With blood dripping out of your ears and your
Fingertips and your tears.
You can have that,
But please go face your fears.
Don't take away my patience.
My patience for you is thin.
If you take one more thing from me,
The balance will be at an end.
And I will no longer be able to,
Hold onto both of our ends.
So keep it down.
Please be quiet.

I'm trying to hold us together.

Let me physically figure it out.

Let me keep us afloat.

Just don't deter me away from our survival,

Just because you don't see an anchor,

That'll hold the boat.

Be quiet.

Or I'll send you away and lock you up again.

Yeah,

Like the last time.

The last, last time.

And all the other time's before then.

4.   Pieces that Died.

Therapist: Tell me about the night that changed everything.

Self: I don't know. So many things, it could've been the last time or maybe the first.

Therapist: A piece of you died that night didn't it? A piece of you left, left you in the cold. Your mind was numb, lips were tight and your eyes were wide from fright. You couldn't even breathe. That's what you said right? Find that night.

Self: Oh... that night. Yeah, the night that changed my heart? A part of my heart just died, left me numb and cold.

Therapist: And your heart? What did you say to the doctors when they told you it was in-operable? That they couldn't make your heart the way it was before?

Self: I told them I knew. That part of me had died along with a chunk of my heart that rotted due to improper care.

Therapist: Now we're getting somewhere. You've finally admitted that part of you has died. Not just your heart. But a part of you. Did you ask the doctors if they could fix that part of you that died? As well as your heart? What they could've done for your being as a whole?

Self: I only care about my heart. And they told me it was in-operable. There was nothing else left to ask.
Therapist: I need to know. Why did you not let the rest of your heart die that night? You could've let go. Do you not believe in Rebirth? You would've had a new heart, a new life. Why are you holding on?

Self: Regeneration. A piece of my heart died that night, rotted off. But the piece of my heart that's still alive believes there's enough light to make my heart whole again.

Therapist: So you believe that there's hope for you? In whole there's hope for your heart? That that piece will grow back in whole?

Self: In time... yes.

Therapist: And the part of you that died as well? Does it regenerate as well?

Self: No. She's dead. She died that night. I don't want her back. I told her I'd take her away if she wouldn't keep quiet. She was too loud and way too damaging to my heart. I had to leave her behind like the last time.

Therapist: So there's no chance she'll come back.

Self: I pray that she holds her silence. But she's made reappearances before. I don't know. She's gone for now and that's all that matters.

Therapist: Do you miss her?

Self: ... She was me, what do you mean? Do I miss apart of myself? A part of myself that I wish would stay dead? What are you asking me? I told you she was gone. I don't want to discuss her anymore. It's 3:00. I only pay you for an hour. Maybe we should talk about this next session.

She abruptly stands and walks away, closing the door behind her softly.

Self: Why did she have to bring her up again?

5.   Heart to Heart Conversations:

Heart: What did you get yourself into?
You fool you fell in love?
The little heart I had left,
You're trying to give to the first giver?
I am your giver!
What do you mean he makes your heart thud?
That's me sitting in your chest!
Naive girl,
Giving it all.
Was it ever yours to give?
You feel whole?
What lies!
That brain of yours must be dead.
PROTECT OUR HEART NO MATTER WHAT!
That was explained at birth.
Here you are stripping slice by slice.
OUR HEART.
TO WHO,
Is that your king?
Will he protect your heart?

Self: Regeneration is the key to fixing our heart.

Love is the only thing that will fix us.

Protect what little we have left?

Why not make ourselves whole?

Faith.

I trust in faith.

Heart: Faith..

You trust in faith.

No, you trust in me.

Pity child.

You fell in love.

You've left us vulnerable.

Vulnerable.

Just know a piece of your heart,

Is going to rot off once again.

Then you'll realize what is making your heart thud.

Pain.

   Pain is making your heart thud.

      Not love.

Naive girl.

6. Regrowth.

Regeneration:
To replace what's lost from within.
Let me reiterate.
Reinvigorate:
To give new energy.
Reclamation:
To take back what was yours.
Reformation:
To correct for growth.
Regeneration not Rebirth.
Reach inside yourself.
That's how it should go.
We all have the ability to grow.
An extension of yourself from yourself.
Like mitosis and meiosis.
A process of growth for oneself.
Regeneration not rebirth.

7. Light Art, Dark Heart.

My heart is tainted with dark shame,
Pain and regrets.
Like glass,
Fine glass,
Antique glass,
Vulnerable glass.
My heart reflected vulnerability.
Slight cracks on the surface,
Varying in size.
But overtime I know the glass will shatter,
Into tiny fine pieces that will,
Cut up my fingers like splinters.
If I tried to pick up the pieces,
My fingers would,
Drip in blood,
Cut up by pieces of myself.
Cut up by past decisions and choices,
That led to shame,
Pain and regrets.
My heart was tainted.
Even my blood began to change.
My heart changed its form,
Deformed with mix colorization.

Some spots bright red,
Glowing in ambition.
And others black like tar,
Rotted.
No longer in commission.
Take care with caution is a label on my heart.
Near the biggest crack in the center,
I pray my dearest plays his part.
I pray his fingers remain unharmed,
When he picks up the pieces,
And rearranges it from the start.
I pray he doesn't get caught up in my decisions,
And my choices that lead me to distraught.
I hope he sees my heart,
Deformed and vulnerable.
But that he also sees art.
I cut up my fingers,
Trying to put the pieces in their correct spots.
But he has a way,
Of handling my shattered heart.
Had a way to stitch my cracks seamless.
He pointed out my flaws,
And called them beautiful.
He gave me pieces of his own heart,
To help mold and weld.
He shaped it with his own hands,

Until it was recognizable as love.
And he put me back together with parts of him,
As bandages to hold my cracks in place,
That he stitched in hopes that I would heal.
He turned my rotted heart into a form of art,
That only he could appreciate.
It was dark.
It was tainted.
But after he had done his part,
He left my heart as art.
He said the outer image of my heart,
Was not an implication,
Of the beauty inside my heart.
That light shines brighter in the darkest pits,
In the darkest corners,
There was always art.

8.   Hotbox 1: Twisted.

Friend: Take a hit of this. I promise it'll get you twisted.

Self: Twisted?

Friend: Yeah man… twisted. More twisted then the shit hovering over your head.

Self: Man, what are you talking about? What twisted shit over my head? You wylin.

Friend: Nah man that twisted shit that's clearly weighing heavy in your head.

Self: ...

Friend: Take a hit of this. I promise it'll get you twisted. It'll have you forgetting all that twisted shit in your head.

Self: ... Yeah, let me get a hit of that. Let me get a few hits of that.

Friend: Just face that shit nigga. Face this blunt, and go about your day. Then go face that twisted shit face to face nigga. Your problems are in your head, you need to face your reality man.

Self: Yeah alright. What you know about facing your problems? Coming at me about my, "make believe," problems, all in my head. Yeah right nigga.

Friend: Bruh, you taking it the wrong way. You ain't heard of the law of attraction? Just smoke this shit and shut up. Let your problems slip out your mind and keep them out is what I'm sayin nigga. Ain't nobody coming for you but YOU nigga. You wanna keep thinking about that negative shit in your head it's gonna start weighing on your shoulders. Gonna start weighing heavy like an anchor in ya head. Ya heard? You're going to start attracting that shit into your life. Straight negativity. Face your reality nigga. Ain't nobody gonna do it for you. And if you can't change shit then find a better way. Think positive shit. You robbin me of my energy right now. How you not know about this?

Self: Yo... yo chill. You went in! Law of attraction? Nigga I'm high as fuck. You been talking and I've been facing this backwood nigga. You telling me all the negative shit in my life I attracted? Same with the positive? The fuck is the law of attraction? Shit sound interesting.

Friend: Nigga I just told you what it was. Man look, there's a book, yo lazy ass can't read go watch the movie on Netflix. It's called, "The Secret."

Self: Whatever man. I'm high as hell I don't even know what we talking about no more.

Friend: Bruh... you just not tryna talk about your problems because you know I'm right. But whatever yo. Stay negative, attract negativity. Change your perspective nigga. Watch how quickly your life will change. Like positive results, you about to pull mad fine bitches too just from your energy.

Self: Bro what the fuck are you talking about.

Friend: Energy nigga. Your energy attracts Other people's aura, I'm telling you.

Self: I'm telling you, you smoking crack. I'm hungry nigga. Faced this backwood I got the munchies.

Friend: Yo don't forget I put you on game when you realize I'm right nigga. Law of attraction is real my guy. You need to start thinking more positive yo. Speak that shit into existence. But aye nigga I'm tired of preaching to your dumb raggedy ass. What you trying to eat fool?

Self: Wendy's, four for four.

Friend: Say less.

9. Mistiming.

I'm not going to make it there in time.
No matter how fast I move,
I know I won't make it.
You're too far.
Way ahead.
I'm nowhere near.
Light years.
How can I explain this?
I thought that I could keep up.
"The Tortoise and the Hare."
But you were lightening.
Too fast,
Like you'd disappear.
I thought I could meet you in time.
But you had ran past the finish line,
And I just so happened to lag behind.
You were gone,
Dust everywhere,
The crowd had disappeared.
I thought that I could make it.
Oh well.
Isolation and despair.

10. Oop's My Bad.

If only you knew.
I almost felt bad.
It was all just a rouse.
How sad.
You thought I meant it?
But then I stabbed.
Stabbed you where it hurts.
Your pride,
Oops my bad.

11. W(hole) Hearted.

She's been wrong about her heart before.
She's held on to her heart,
As an incomplete whole.
Afraid to be left a little uncomfortable.
With a gaping hole in her chest.
She thought that it would grow.
That incomplete whole,
That hole,
That gaping hole.
She tried to fill it for some time.
But found she was drowning overtime.
She had stepped out of line.
Her heart was half and she had holes.
She wanted to grow flowers,
In the holes of her heart.
She packed the spots with soft dirt,
And added some seeds.
In hopes some beauty would grow within.
Instead of watering her holes with H20,
In hopes flowers would bloom beautiful.
She watered her holes,
When she was feeling less whole,
With spirits and fine wine.

She had already overflowed.
And overtime the seeds died,
The dirt dried fast.
Her holes were left uncovered.
Her heart never recovered.
And she was still left,
Un-whole.

12. No Peeks.

I haven't looked back to my past in a while.
I left it behind.
Over my shoulder,
No peeks.
It hurt for a while.
I was always side glancing,
Under eye.
I watched behind me so often.
I got stuck in my head,
Stuck in my past.
I watched myself past my peak.
But setback,
Opaque.
Getting stuck in my head,
I found that I was weak.
Weak,
So weak.
But now my eyes stay forward.
Reach new heights and new peaks.
Find confidence in myself.
Positivity,
New reach.
My eyes stay forward towards,
My present,
My future and my new peak.
No more looking back.
I'm trying not to be weak.
To be weak when I reach my peak,
Will have me falling down to my knees.
I stopped looking back,

Never over my shoulder,
No looks.
No peeks.
Just straight forward,
Toward a new me.

13. Death Feigning.

Just the word itself is so enticing.
On my lips,
I play with the way it sounds.
So sexy.
"Death."
And you would think it would send shivers,
Down my spine.
Instead,
It pushes blood through my being.
Straight to my chest,
To my cheeks.
A blush.
A brush with death.
Has my heart beating.
Death,
Oh death.
God,
I wish I wasn't breathing.
Just for a second.
So that I could embrace the warmth momentarily.
That comes with death.
Maybe I'm a little dead already.
But does it make me morbid?

That I'm attracted to death?
That when the Reaper comes,
I'll ask him to be my first dance.
I'll ask him to lead the steps.
Like the first dance,
The first steps.
A wedding with death,
Sounds lovely.
At the alter I'll ask the Reaper,
If he'll become my keeper.
He'll say yes,
And my chest will explode.
He'll lean in to seal the deal and wait,
In hopes that I'll accept his will.
I do.
I do accept.
Yes,
Oh yes,
Oh Reaper I do accept!
Go ahead and give me,
The kiss of death.

14. Moral Compass

Do you know your right from wrong?
The same way you know your lefts from your right?
Do you know your voice carries weight?
So, watch what you say.
And when you're going to be late,
Do you call or do you make me wait?
Did you see me crying quietly?
Or did you look away without counseling?
If I told you I was down,
Would you care?
Or would you tell me it's all in my head.
You noticed I stopped eating,
But you didn't speak up.
I guess it's not your business,
If I go and throw up.
Did you pay attention when I said that,
Death was awaiting?
Or were your ears tuned into a different
conversation?
Your moral compass for me has to be broken,
Or you're oblivious to my suffers.
Cause you won't check in to say,

"What's wrong? Was it something I said? I'm sorry. I should've told you, 'I'm running a bit late. I'm sorry I made you wait.' I noticed you were crying. Oh honey, don't you know you're great? But you have to eat, don't throw it all away. And death? Yeah, he's coming when you're old, frail and lived up to date. Don't worry, I'm here, watching. Listen, you're not a mistake."

But your moral compass is broken.
You're never going to notice.
Oblivious to my sufferings.
A blind eye to my pain.
Oh well,
Too late.
By the time your eyes are open,
I'll be gone,
Ashes,
Dust,
Bones,
And pain.
Oblivious to my sufferings.
You left me in disdain.

15: Voiceless Vibrations.

The way my heart beats,
For you,
So erratically,
Through my chest.
I can feel the,
Love,
Pain,
And regrets.
Through every breath.
And sometimes I catch my words,
Slipping slowly,
Stuck in my chest.
I wish I had a voice.
Yet I let you walk by,
To the beat of your own drum.
The drum that matches my heartbeats.
Bum,

                Bum,

                                Bum.

I wish that I could tell you.
The way my chests beats.

                                Pat,

                Pat,

Pat.

When you're in my presence.
The way my heart beats for you,
Craving your very essence.
I wonder if,
You can feel the vibrations,
Coming from my chest?
If you laid your bare hands over my heart,
"X marks the spot."
You would feel the,
Love,
Pain,
Regrets.
Through every breathe.
You would feel the,
Words slipping slowly down my neck.
I guess,
My voice will forever be stuck in my chest.
With you never having a second guess.

16. Fast Forward, Flat line.

Everything is wrong,
A disaster,
A mess.
A tornado twisted over my head.
It's my fault I guess,
See I do this often.
I wallow in distress,
Depressed.
I let it take over and make a mess,
A mess in every aspect.
I can't seem to make the best,
The best decisions.
The less choices I possess,
The less my mind is aware of my steps.
My steps.
Lead in one direction.
Backwards.
Pressed.
Like my legs pressed backwards.
I watch my life move forward.
But my legs.
My legs move back in time,
Stuck in rewind.

Stuck in time.

But I guess I never learned,

You can't press rewind in real life,

To save yourself.

So, I guess I'll have to just,

Press fast forward,

Flat line,

Guess I'll just have to end myself.

17. That's How We Actin' Now?

Somebody that I used to know: Don't be like that.
Don't act like I never had you like that.
Can't believe you put my name in your mouth,
And you spit it out like that.
Have me real lost.
Have me feeling crossed.
Can't believe you're even acting out like that.
Fact check me if I'm wrong,
You weren't built like that.
You were built from love,
You were made like that.
So, tell me what's up?
Why you changed like that?
Why you sitting here,
Spitting game like that?
That's what I taught you?
Maybe I'm the one to blame for that.
You adopted my ways,
Girl,
That's why I fear you like that.
You the only one,
That could have me weary like that.
So maybe my lack of love,

Is making you act like that.
But you know I always had you.
Put your guard back down,
Baby I loved you better like that.
I'll treat you better now,
For a fact.
If you'll hold me close,
And tell me you want me right back.
Give me another chance,
You know I got you like that.
I promise I'll kiss you slow,
I'll love you better,
But you can't act out like that.
Just don't leave me out in the cold.
Cause I would never treat you like that.

Self: You had your chance,
And you left.
You broke apart of me,
And you left.
You messed with my head,
Made me feel wanted,
And you left.
Your words are just words.
Words that I've fallen for before.
And even then,

When I forgave you,
Time and time again,
You left.
Your words carry no weight.
That's why I left.
I'm not falling for it.
You'll just have to be misfortunate.

Somebody that I used to know: Oh,
So that's how we acting now?
You acting flaw.
You're done?
Just like that?
You're gonna keep your guard up,
Not let me in like that?
I guess you adopted my ways.
I guess we're ending like that.

Self: Yeah,
I hope you know you changed my heart,
For the worst.
Now I'm picking up the pieces,
Trying to make myself work.
Please leave me alone,
Please don't ever reach out.
Don't ever come back.

I'm leaving you in the past.

And yeah.

I guess we are ending just like that.

18. Lies Told at Home.

I told you I wanted to go home.
Well I meant I wanted to go into your arms.
You quickly added and intervened.
"I am your home,
My arms would always find you."
And in my mind,
I nearly cried.
I felt the love inside me.
You told me I was your place to lie.
You'd love to devour me nicely.
You said that I owned your heart,
And not to lose its value.
I owned a part of you,
You owned everything inside me.
I knew that I had found the one,
When home was arms and manly cologne.
Wrapped nice and really tightly,
Around my waist,
With lips to taste.
And all I could put into words was that,
I had finally found my lifeline.
And I was done being lost,
No more,

Not likely.

I'll follow your voice and it'll lead me to home.

Where you'll be,

And you'll wrap your arms around me.

You are my home it seems.

But you weren't,

You were a wolf in sheep's clothing,

Promising me a home,

Even when I was just your last meal,

I was never your lifeline.

19. Giving Up on Love.

I can feel,

My heart slipping,

Back into its old ways.

It's used to lots of love and care.

But now you've gone away.

It's hard to say this,

But my heart is in dismay.

You used to care.

You used to fill my heart with love.

But now it's empty.

Like four bare walls,

With no furniture,

No home.

No visitors or loved ones.

I used to carry lots of love,

But now I'm running empty.

Just the word itself,

Doesn't sound appealing.

I don't believe in love anymore,

Not for me anyways.

They come and go,

And say their piece,

And lure me in,

Then leave me.
So, I'm done with love.
An empty casket,
My heart no longer beating.

20. New Text Message.

Unread Message:

Luvr: I just don't want to talk to you, at all. I'm not going to sit here and pretend I do. I don't see the point in anything right now with you. I can't do us right now. I'm just doing me right now and it's nothing against you. I'm just going through some things that I have to handle without you.
1:38 PM

Sent Message:

Self: Wait what? Baby.. where did I go wrong?
1:40 PM

Unread Message:

Luvr: I don't want to talk. There was never a plan for you. I took this too far and now I'm out.
2:47 PM

Sent Message:

Self: I don't understand. No plan for me? What about everything we planned for? You're my home. Baby please talk to me.
2:49 PM

Unread Message:

Luvr: Look you can't make me talk to you. Clearly, I don't want to. I can't talk right now.
3:03 PM

Sent Message:

Self: Wait no... You can't just leave, not after everything we've done. You can't just ice me out and leave me out in the cold. I have no idea what's going on. What about our love? What about life without you? How do you expect me to do this without you?
MESSEGE NOT DELIVERED.
3:05 PM

Realize your message was never delivered and not just through text. You lost your Luvr just like that but you'd been blind to his disguise for years. Your message was never received, your love went to waste and he won't be here to watch you recover.

21. Luvr Had to Go.

Where did my Luvr go?
Over the moon,
Did he jump and go?
Like the river,
Did he follow his own flow?
Oh where did my Luvr go?
Is he my luvr or my foe?
Seems to be one or the other,
His mood decides if he goes.
Where did my luvr go?
Did you see him past?
Oh, you've never met my last Luvr...
So he could disappear and nobody would ever
Notice him pass by?
Except me...
I guess that's what you get.
When you love undercover.
Your Luvr can leave like leaves blowing under.
With nobody to spot him.
And your heart left to never recover.

22. MRS.RAGER

How does it feel,
To breathe,
The pain inside you?
Does it sting?
Does it burn?
Is your breath hot inside you?
Do you plan on extinguishing the fire?
Or sitting underneath it so you can finally feel,
Feel some kind of feeling that makes you feel
Something,
For once.
I hope you'll finally feel it.
I hope you'll finally find it,
The fire that's been raging for years,
Inside you.
MRS.RAGER,
Are you going to face your fears?

23. No Next Time.

Goodbyes are getting old.
I'm getting tired of begging you not to go.
Next time go ahead and go.
Next time go ahead and fold.
This relationship is full of so much hatred.
Next time don't even try and hold,
My hand.
Just leave me alone.
For good.
Because you thought I wasn't enough.
Now you want to make love to me?
Cry me a river,
Then swim in it.
And drown in your regrets.
And leave me,
Just forget,
Because goodbyes are getting old.
Next time,
Just know.
That no means no.
Just go ahead and go.
I'm not holding you here,
Anymore

24. Words Cut Deep.

Feeling's too deep.
>> Cut too deep.
>>> I don't need no knifes,

Or pointy thing's.
>> Sticks and stones,
>>> Will break my bones.

But words will break my soul.
>> Feeling too deep.
>>> My hole is too steep.

Don't need nobody to control me.
>> I'm stuck in this hole.
>>> I'm stuck in this rut.

Nobody is going to save me.

25. Leave Your Message at the Beep.

Ring.

Ring.

Ring.

Ring.

Ring.

Ring.

Ring.

Automated message: "The mailbox you dialed cannot be reached at this time. Please leave your message for _____ at the beep. When you are finished recording, please hang up. Or press # for more options."

Beep.

Self: "Hey,

It's me.

Um,

I'm not sure what to say.

I knew you wouldn't answer,

I wanted to reach your voicemail.

And I did.

But now that I have,

I forgot what to say.

I haven't heard from you in a while.

I guess I just wanted to make sure you were ok.

But I guess that's not enough of a reason,

To call now-a-days.

I wanted to know if you missed me,

The same way I've been missing you.

And I wanted to tell you,

That I loved you so much.

I wish that you could've knew.

Would've saw,

How much I needed you.

You know,

Honestly.

You left me in the cold.

You told me I was, "your everything."

I guess you just had to fold.

You know,

I'm actually kind of pissed.

You took me as a joke.

How could you use me like this?

And leave me by my lonely.

God,

It's been days and you're still radio silent.

I know you've seen the texts and calls.

You're just choosing to remain silent.

You're just choosing to ignore me.

I don't know why my emotions still control me.

You don't even know me anymore.

We're strangers.

Yet I still want you to know me.

And it isn't fair,

That you casted a spell,

And latched me on your body.

Because now I'm left,

To live all by my lonely.

I wish that I had never fell,

For you...

This hurts too much I can't...

Self: #

Automated message:

Press one to send your message.

Press two to hear your message over.

Press three to send with urgency.
Press four to continue recording.
Press five to erase and start over.
Press six to erase and cancel.

Self: Six.

Beep.

Automated Message:
Your message has been erased.
Goodbye.

End call.

Self: Calm down.
You're caught up in your emotions.
Just breathe.
He doesn't even deserve,
To hear you speak well of him.
Stop telling him,
You love him.
You've got to stop acting out on a whim.
If he's not the one for you,
You'll live.
Go back to pretending.

Don't let your mind control you.

It's a battle between your heart and your mind.

Your wants and needs.

You don't need him.

You wanted him.

Wants do not beat our needs.

Remember that please.

He was just here for a time.

Your mind and heart will always find a way to heal.

Even without him here to stay.

26. Foreclosure.

57

I wanted to go home,
Well I meant into your arms.
But now I realized I was homeless.
I had no place I belonged.
No hand or heart to own.
My home was you,
But now you're gone.

27. Soul Tied.

How many times has my soul,
Been tied off to dead weight?
How many times did I pour my heart out?
Just to be told to wait,
That your love would always be late.
That you would never be there the way,
I wanted you to be.
But how can I,
Keep coming back?
The way that I have,
For you.
Forgiving you.
Allowing you back in.
Allowing my heart to crack,
Every time that you left.
But whenever you came back,
It was like heaven again.
Soul ties.
My soul was tied to you.
Every time we intertwined,
I gave you part of me.
You took a part of me,
And gave me nothing in return.

Yet I still gave to you, everything.
I guess I didn't mean as much to you,
The way you meant to me.
You left,
Not realizing my soul was tied to yours.
And now you won't respond.
Won't return what was mine.
My soul and light,
That you robbed right out of my body.

28. No More Light.

60

I have,
No more light.
In the,
Crevices of,
My heart.
All the,
Light,
Dissipated.
Darkness,
In,
Every,
Corner.
No more light.
All my,
Lights,
Seemed to,
Dim.
I have,
No more light,
In my heart.
Just,
Darkness.

29. Puzzle Pieces.

Trying to find love in everything,
I lost myself trying to give love to everyone.
I lost myself trying to be everything,
For everyone else,
But myself.
Can't,
Seem,
To,
Find,
Myself,
Ever again.
Can't,
Seem,
To,
Be,
There,
For myself.
I'm lonely.
The kind of lonely,
That another human,
Can't fix.
The,
Kind,
Of,
Lonely,
You feel,
When you feel,
Alone,
From yourself.
Keep trying to fix myself.

Thought our,
Broken pieces,
Would connect,
Like puzzle pieces...
But I guess,
Our puzzle pieces,
Was never meant to be completed.
The picture was never created.
Only because,
My puzzles pieces,
Couldn't connect.
To my own,
Heart.
Scattered.
The puzzle,
My puzzle,
Was never,
Meant to,
Be,
Touched.
Or,
Loved.
My puzzle pieces,
Could,
Never,
Connect.
I could,
Never,
Complete,
A picture,
With you.
I will,
Never,

Connect,
With anyone,
And not just you.
My incomplete puzzle pieces,
Will never,
Fit,
With anyone.
Alone.
I lost some,
Puzzle pieces,
I'll never,
Complete the picture,
Of my,
Heart.
Of my,
Soul.
Of,
Myself.
I am lost.
No pieces to be connected.
No picture to ever be created.

30. Pseudo Love.

I don't want to be your sometime.
Your go to when you are down.
But you disappear after you're done,
Girl.
I don't want to be your rebound.
"I'm settling for now but soon I'm leaving,"
Girl.
I don't want to be your home,
If you're only renting.
If you are not mine to own.
I'll give up the deed then.
I don't want no indecisive cheap clown.
No inconsistent feelings now.
You're holding out cause,
You see no future now?
But sold me to the dream,
Wow!
You're taking it back?
No Walt Disney now?
I don't want no lies,
No false prophets.
Instead of selling me to your reality,
You sold me to the dream.
I don't want false love,
False promises,
False trust.
Not only lust.
I wanted real love.
That real love that brings you peace.
The type that makes you fear love if it ever leaves.

But I'm just your sometime,
Your,
"I'm feeling down,
Can you come around then I'm leaving,"
Girl.
I'm just a rebound,
Your now-a-later,
Your free tour.
Your lust toy.
Your lease renting co-owner.
I am not your home.
Nor your doormat.
Nor do I want that.
I wanted love,
You gave me lust.
You gave me sometimes.
I want to be yours.
But I don't want no fake love,
No maybe love,
No good for my brain love.
I don't want your definition of love.
It's all games is what it was.
So please back the fuck up.
I've finally found what I was looking for.
Stability.
Consistency.
I found that love in myself.

31. Get Up 10.

Did it again.
I fell again.
Fall down 8,
But I get up 10.
Seem to,
Pretend.
Can't really,
Retain,
How I did it again.
Fell down 8,
But I got up 10.
Thought I was gonna,
Let it sink in,
All of this mental depression.
But I beat it again,
Fall down 8,
Get up 10.

32. Count Down Methods.

I was taught,

That if I was ever,

Feeling scared, anxious or nervous.

I should count down from 10,

To release stress and angst.

A method I learned from my own Therapist and Psychiatrist.

But when I count down from 10

It goes a lot more like this:

10:

Breathe in.

9:

Breathe out.

8:

Inhale.

7:

Exhale.

6:

Hold your breathe.

5:

Rooms spinning.

4:

Panic.

3:

Dizzy.

2:

Seeing nothing.

1:

Unconscious.

There's a lot of Countdown Methods,
For people like me.
Who are diagnosed with:
Bi-Polar Depression, Panic Disorder, Acute Anxiety
And prone to attacks,
At any moment.
Counting down from 10,
Doesn't work.
It was never good,
For,
My,
Conscious Sanity.
Until then,
My,
Mind will remain,
Unconscious and insane.
With too many thoughts crowding,

Every corner of my brain.
No amount of counting,
Would ever make them go away.

33. Hired Gun.

Head spinning.
Mind numb.
Crazy feeling.
Hired gun.
Sent him here.
With a hand gun.
Take my life.
Fire gun.
Take my life.
I am not the one,
To turn my life around.
I am done.
Paid him off.
No tracking gun.
Tell him off,
If he misses the shot.
Only got one target.
Aim straight.
To my head.
Take a hit.
I am not the one.
Surely I would hope,
To be gone.
Hired gun.
Target one.
Aim straight to my cranium.

34. Giving Up.

Leaving my voice behind.
Leaving my mind behind.
Leaving my love behind.
Leaving my lust behind.
Leaving it all behind.
Can it stay there?
Away from me in another dimension?
Where my love isn't needed?
Where no thinking is needed?
Where nonspeaking is needed?
Where lust turns into more than needed?
Will I see it?
Sky wise,
Will it be blue?
Like earth,
Will this new earth supply me,
Of what I'm lacking?
Not likely.
No earth supplies me,
Of the world I am lacking.
I guess we travel,
To find new places,
That accept us.
But find that,
No place supplies us,
Of the happiness,
We crave.
Of the love we base our hearts on.
Will you accept our grace or turn your,
Back around and neglect us access to,

What we need?
Will we rot instead,
Lacking of the love we seeked?
Will time fly by like it never existed?
Will we drift into an abyss?
An abyss we'll never escape.
Our happiness,
Will never,
Reach the stars,
The galaxies,
Like we dreamed.
A distant day dream is what we only reach,
Never breaking past something meant to be.

35. Too Much Value.

I understand now.
I was too much for you.
My damaged heart,
Was too much for you.
I gave you all the love in me.
Even though there were all these holes,
In my less than whole heart.
I understand now.
It wasn't me,
It was you.
A coward.
A coward with no heart.
Who told me I had no part,
In his life.
But it wasn't me.
I understand now.
My love is too much for you.
My being is too much for you.
My very essence screams value.
That you could never afford.
I understand now.
You always knew you could never afford me.
Not something of this value.
It wasn't me.
It was you.

36. She Was.

She used to fly with,
Hummingbirds,
And,
Blue jays.
She swam with,
Dolphins,
And,
Mermaids.
She ran with,
The lions,
And,
Cheetahs.
Queen of the Forest,
Queen of the Sea,
Queen of the Sky,
Queen of the Universe.
She aimed for the sky.
The stars.
She was beauty.
A level headed queen.
A master piece.
She was.

She was.

And then she wasn't.

37. Baby Bird Blue.

Baby bird blue.
Baby bird,
You know you.
Better than your own mother do.
Baby bird knew,
She knew if she flew,
She would never turn back.
And would always move,
In the direction of the wind.
Her mother knew this sadly.
So she clipped her wings.
She never taught baby blue to,
Flap her wings.
But baby bird blue,
Baby bird knew,
She had to go soon.
Her mother had left,
Searching for food.
So baby bird stood tall,
At the edge of her nest.
Her baby bird siblings prayed she'd do her best.
They knew her wings were clipped,
And that she had never flew.
But baby bird blue said goodbye nonetheless,
Then she dived.
Free falling.
Face forward.
Her wings didn't grab air.
Baby bird blue descended fast.
But before she hit the ground,

SPLAT!
She heard her mother yell.
"Blue no!
I don't want to lose you.
Flap your wings and fly baby blue!
I know I never taught you but flying it's in you!"
And in the last second,
Baby bird blue flapped her wings hard.
So hard, her wings took wind and she flew.
She flapped and flapped until she rose.
She flew to her mother.
Proclaimed,
"I love you, but I must go find my own view."
She pecked her mother goodbye,
And wrapped her wing
Around her baby bird siblings.
Then, baby bird blue took off again,
And she flew and flew.
Baby bird blue was gone.
And her mother didn't know what to do.
She'd grown up.
Left the nest.
She flew.
And baby bird never looked back.
She flew and flew.
With the sun to her back.
Hitting her wings.
Never having a clue,
About how cruel the real world would be.

38. Missing.

I miss you.
More than I've missed anything.
I crave you,
Your very skin.
Your fingertips against,
My temple running down my face.
I miss your kiss.
Your caress.
I miss your breathe,
Against the nape of my neck.
I miss your voice.
And your laughter,
Was always like a melody.
A beautiful tone stuck in my head.
It's a tragedy.
I miss the way you didn't leave.
I hate that you became the very,
Dream I was trying to achieve.
You showed me life and gave me energy,
And sooner than later you were gone,
Like my sanity.
I miss you,
Your very being.
But now I see,
What I was always meant to see.
Your underlying truth.
The picture was perfect with just you.
No place for me.
I was always a liability.
Expendable and never a priority.

I miss you.
But my voice will have to be,
Trapped inside of me.
No speaking up.
No more traveling.
The little heart that's left,
Is in catastrophe.
Pieces hanging off,
Rotted holes inside of me.
I miss you.
Because you took half of me.
My heart.
My soul that's tied off to yours.
My voice.
My ability to ever love again.
You took it with you,
And claimed it was for good riddance.

I miss you.
I miss the part of me,
That you took from me.
I miss me more than anything.
Who am I?
You see.
I am "She."
I am you.
I am your luvr,
I am your best friend,
Your mother,
Your feelings,
Your mind,
Your heart,
Your unheard voice.

I am "She."
I am nobody.
I am everyone.
I am your peace of mind.
Your conscious,
Sigmund Freud Id,
Unconscious mind.
I am everything.
I am nothing.
A black hole.
An endless sea.
I am love,
And despair.
Light and dark matter.
You have not experienced all of me,
What's inside me,
To understand what is missing.
To understand what you robbed out of me.
You left me empty and alone with no way,
Of ever fixing me.

39. Butterflies.

Sweet butterflies,
In my stomach again.
Eyes lock,
Blood running again.
Take it slow,
No running again.
Don't question the flow.
But remember not to pretend.
Butterflies flying again.
In my tummy,
When you're looking at me.
Remember,
Not to give too much of me to you.
Like the last time,
And that blew.
No more pieces to give.
Too many holes in my heart.
But the butterflies,
In my stomach.
Sweet butterflies,
Flying again.
Remind me that,
There would always be light inside of me.
A feeling I'd love to feel again

40. Fine Before You.

Little pieces of today,
That still remind me of yesterday.
Still stuck in the past,
Still stuck in this mental state,
Where everything was still you.
Less of me.
Less is all that's left.
Little pieces of you etched into,
My mental,
There's a clear image of you.
Day by day trying to make more of me,
But don't want to lose the little of you,
I'm holding onto.
No idea who I really am anymore.
A monster with no heart?
Who was never trained to love the right way?
I became my worst nightmare.
Trying to be with you.
Now all I have is less of me,
And too much of you.
Adopted your ways,
A monster with no heart,
Who was trained to break hearts.

Just games played by the puppet master,
I adopted your ways,
I became the female version of you.
Shame,
I was perfectly fine before you.

41. Pretend.

Unkempt hair like a nest.
Pass your hand over your face like a mask,
And smile.
Wipe the tears from your eyes.
Take down your hair,
And comb it through.
Smile through it all.
Apply make-up.
No one will even notice,
How much of a mess,
You really are,
Inside.
Easier to pretend.
Pretend like you feel the same.
Knowing all you feel is pain.
Smile,
And hold it in.
Nobody has to see your pain within.
Except you.

42. "Heart" to Heart Conversations: Faith Is Your Enemy.

Heart: I told you this would happen.
Now you're in dismay.
You cannot see after.
There's nothing left in your bay.
I told you giving more,
Then reciprocated,
Would lead our heart to war.
With grenades leaving massive craters,
Blown to bits in our caved heart.
I told you.
And I told you again.
That he would not give you after.
Or the happiness that you crave.
Your heart will not grow,
Nor light shine through.
I told you preservation,
Was the only way to go.
You claimed regeneration,
Was the one thing that would show,
That would lead the way to being whole.
Not realizing we had too many holes.
Holes that I was managing.
Before you lost control.

Now you see,
I told you.
To take care,
Protect me.
And you didn't.
Left us less than whole,
Left us with more than we could handle.
Now you're here telling me,
You have everything under control?
Tell me?
What's the plan?
How many more holes,
Do you think our heart can take?
Before it collapses in on itself?
No redemption.
For your sake,
I'd give up.
No regeneration.

Self: All you can say is, "I told you so."
You give me no praise.
I'm holding us up.
Pray you see that,
Being alone will bring us nothing but pain.
I hope you realize,
That I am filled with light.

Preservation isn't my game.

I claimed regeneration.

Reformation.

He left.

But he was not my light.

I create my own healing light.

I trust in faith.

Heart: Pity child.

> When will you realize that faith,

>> Is your enemy?

43. Daily Reminders.

Remember,
Not to feel too much.
Live in the moment.
Keep certain things untouched.
And have no expectations,
From anyone.
How not to get disappointed,
And not lose too much.

44. Nothing Changed.

Nothing was the same.
But it was.
The wind blew softly.
And the leaves still began,
To change their colors.
Time continued.
The summer's heat,
Was still ripe over our heads.
Nothing changed.
Not physically.
A mask I wore day by day.
For strangers and friends.
No.
Nothing changed.
Because on the inside.
I was still dead.

45. Actions and Words.

Feeling like anything can happen,
Loving the way things are going.
But know that it's only temporary.
Feeling like I'm out of pocket,
With the things I do,
The things I say.
My actions speak louder than my words.
Or should I say my lack of action,
Speaks louder than most.
Loving the way things are going.
Loving the flow.
But my rivers overflowed.
And I realize I cannot take anymore.
Drowning in my own actions and words.
You're better off without me.
Build my walls so high,
Like the Eiffel Tower,
And the Great Wall of China.
Hopefully you don't see right through my bluff.
And realize what kind of person I am.
The kind of person with too much holes.
Whose walls were held up like a fortress.
Protecting ourselves in hopes,
We'll remain whole.

46. Home is Where My Heart Beats.

Played me like a violin,

Until I bled your favorite song.

Played me til' I was numb,

No feelings left undone.

Everything seemed at bliss.

But it seems our love was broken.

Nobody to call my own.

No home to lay my head in.

You've found better,

She's more than I could ever fathom.

I'll never be like them.

I'll never lay beside your head,

And hear your soft voice.

I won't get to hold your hand,

And tell everyone you're the one.

Though those are the only things,

I'd be missing.

Nothing with substance like trust,

Faith and permission.

Thank God,

They don't outweigh the good.

The good,

Where I am happy.

Where I am smiling for no one,
But myself.
Where I can say I did it on my own.
I held up myself,
And let the light shine through.
I'll love the new person I'm becoming,
Because of you,
Because you left.
Because of the pain you caused me,
That changed my very being.
Yet I'm here.
Standing tall,
Still aware of my guard.
I gained some pride,
Some confidence and stride.
Something I never had with you.
But now I'm all I got.
Home is where my heart resides.
I no longer need your doubt.
Home is where my hallowed chambers,
Hold a holed,
Less than whole,
Heart.
Home is where I am.
Where light resides,
In the deepest darkest corner of my chambers.

You taught me light shines brighter,
In the darkest hearts.
And it did.
I found home.
Home is where my light doesn't dim.
Home is where a dark heart binds with light.
Pure light.
Home is light inside of me.
Home is where my heart beats.
And I am the only one,
With the way into my home.
My heart beat being the combination to home.
Home is inside of me.
Not inside of anyone.

47. Sometimes.

Sometimes,
I weep.
Sometimes,
I seep myself,
In heat.
In hate.
In love.
Sometimes,
I fall,
Sometimes,
I break.
And sometimes,
I pick up my pieces,
And put myself together.
But then...
I break again.
And sometimes,
My pieces break too much.
And I can't put myself back together.
Sometimes,
I create,
A new image of me.
A pretend me,
An okay me.
And for a while,
Sometimes,
It works.
But sometimes,

Most times,
It does until,
It doesn't.

48. Dying Wish.

My only dying wish,
Is one where your lips,
Touch mine,
One more time.
Not even the kiss,
But the feeling it up brings.
Of warmth and content.
I want to embrace,
This feeling,
All the time.
From dawn to dusk.
Endlessly until I lay my head to rest.
The feeling you bring,
Inside of me.
The feeling of love that uplifts me.
The feeling of warmth and content,
That consumes me.
Consumes me in love.
I wish for my final wish,
Before I lay my head to rest.
I wish for love,
Endless love,
An endless kiss,
Until I lay my head to rest,
To live in an eternity of bliss.
Pure Bliss.
My final dying wish,
Is that,
Of love,
Warmth,

And something more,
Than just your lips.

49. Lie To Rest.

How can I keep telling myself,
I'm ready for this,
Or that I'm ready for anything?
When my life's a mess,
And my heart is holed.
I cannot hold anything in my heart,
Fall out the holes like Swiss.
How can I keep telling myself,
My life is whole and filled with light?
When all I see is darkness.
When all I breathe is toxic waste.
I cannot see nor taste greatness.
How can I ask of you,
To fill me with your praise?
If I cannot praise myself,
Nor love myself fully.
Like the beautiful person that I am.
I cannot see nor hear my legacy.
How can I be anything new,
If I refuse to grow and bloom?
When I refuse all the opportunities,
That surround me in fear,
Of rejection and distaste.
I cannot plant my seed nor my roots,
In hopes flowers would bloom beautiful.
I am twisted.
In a way that excludes me from other women,
From other humans at that.
My inclusion of myself does not exist.
I cannot carry the weight of the world.

And handle my plate.
Excluding me from my faith.
No need to dwell in my past.
Knowing my present form here,
Will not lead to a future.
I cannot promise you I will be here.
Or there in my future form.
Nor can I say that,
I won't be the cause of my dismay.
I cannot speak nor show you my pain.
You're better off not listening.
Not looking.

Not speaking of me.
I will become a distant memory,
When I'm gone.
Only self-medicating therapy,
Will make me feel strong.
I must feel empty.
I cannot say I will be here,
Or there,
In my future form.
So see me now,
In the present time.
Hear me now.
Feel me now.
Deep in my emotions.
Claw me out of my despair.
Show me why I have to be there,
In my future form.
But will you promise me that you'll be there?
To hold my hand every step of the way?
That's something you can't say.

It seems I can only commit,
To my untimely death.
I can only commit to a future,
Where my death is imminent and red.
I cannot see day nor the nights stars.
May we lay my head to rest.

50. Mary.

Mary,
Mary may I?
Mary may I get a puff?
Can I smoke ya?
Til' my mind is numb.
Til' my pain is dim.
Til' all I feel is you?
Mary Jane?
My best friend.
The only feeling,
I let within.
You feed my soul.
My sanity.
Stop the attacks,
My body feeds me.
You,
Every puff,
Inhaling deep.
You are my peace.
The only thing,
That has stopped me,
From me.

51. Baggage.

I wish I never gave you a part of me. I gave you
the part of me that allowed love and light into me. I
gave it all to you. Now I'm feeling all these blues.
And I tried to give a part of me to someone more
deserving but I had nothing left to give. You took
too much and left me restless. You were the first
person to show me my light but you had to break
me first to get me there. Your love was never real
and our soul tie left me damaged. But some good
did come out of it, I found my worth and value.

www.ingramcontent.com/pod-product-compliance
Lightning Source LLC
Chambersburg PA
CBHW051441150726
48000CB00005B/2198